THE WATER OF LIFE

BY JAY & VICTORIA
WILLIAMS

ILLUSTRATED BY
LUCINDA McQUEEN

HAZELDEN

Published originally by Four Winds Press 1980.
First published by Hazelden Foundation October 1990.

ISBN: 0-89486-721-0

Library of Congress Catalog Card Number:
90-82997

Printed in the United States of America.

Editor's note:

Hazelden Educational Materials offers a variety of information on chemical dependency and related areas. Our publications do not necessarily represent Hazelden or its programs, nor do they officially speak for any Twelve Step organization.

THE
WATER
OF
LIFE

ilchard the fisherman was known as a helpful man. He lived in a snug cottage beside the river and spent his days fishing or working in his garden, but he was always ready to give a neighbor a hand. What fish he couldn't eat, he sold for a penny, and when he had an extra penny, he gave it away to someone who needed it. When someone was hungry, there was always a cabbage or a bunch of carrots to spare from Pilchard's garden. If a roof needed shingling, Pilchard would help shingle it; if a boat needed mending, Pilchard would help mend it.

His friend Tompkin said to him, "You spend all your time helping others, and you have nothing left for yourself."

But Pilchard just laughed. "I've got a house, and a garden, and a river to fish in," said he. "And I can give a friend a hand and still have two left."

One day, a message came from the king, summoning Pilchard to the castle at once. Pilchard washed the fish scales off his hands, put on his best coat, and trudged up the hill to the castle.

The king was sitting in a golden rocking chair, smoking a long pipe. He was wearing his second-best crown, which was not as heavy as the other one.

"Pilchard," he said, "I hear you are a helpful man."

"So they say, Your Majesty," said Pilchard, with a bow.

"Good," said the king. "I want you to help me."

Pilchard looked around the room in surprise. The walls were of silver, and the lamps were cut out of solid diamonds.

"How can I help you?" he said. "You've got everything fit for a king."

"Not everything," said the king, with a sigh. "What I want more than anything in the world is the Water of Life."

"What is that, Your Majesty?"

"Ah, Pilchard," said the king, "just thinking about it makes me feel happy. It gives health and joy. If you are ill, it makes you feel better. A few drops, and everything around you becomes beautiful. He who has the Water of Life needs nothing else."

He put down his pipe. "Pilchard," he said, "bring me the Water of Life, and I will give you whatever you wish."

Pilchard scratched his head. "Well, well," said he, "if you want it that badly, I'll have to help you. Where is this wonderful stuff?"

"That's just the trouble, don't you see?" said the king. "Nobody knows."

Pilchard thought for a moment. "All right," he said, "I'll set out at once."

"Which way will you go?" asked the king.

"If nobody knows where it is," said Pilchard, "then one direction is as good as another. But if no one knows where it is, then it must be in some place where no one ever goes. So that's where I'll go."

He went home and packed up some bread and cheese and his fishing line. He said good-bye to all his neighbors and told them to help themselves from his garden. He looked around once at all the friendly, familiar things, and set off.

He wandered for many days, over rough hills and through pleasant valleys. He went where no one ever went, and after a long time he found himself at the edge of a forest. Among the tree trunks lay dark shadows. A sad wind stirred the leaves.

Pilchard turned up his coat collar. "Just the place!" he said cheerfully. "Surely, no one ever comes *here*."

He stepped boldly into the forest. He marched along under the branches, and at last he came to a clearing where there was a huge oak tree. Something moved among the shadows. Pilchard stopped.

There, under the tree, was a strange beast, long and scaly like a serpent but with the legs and head of an eagle. Four wings drooped at its sides. Its eyes were as cold as pebbles, but it did not look directly at Pilchard, only sideways, from the corners of its eyes. It was a basilisk.

That was the first thing Pilchard saw. The second thing he saw was that it was tied to the tree by a rope.

"Poor thing!" said Pilchard, before he could stop himself.

"What?" said the basilisk, in a grating voice. "I have not heard a word of pity since I was tied to this tree, five hundred years ago."

"Who tied you there?" asked Pilchard.

"A great magician who came when the people of the kingdom complained about me. If you had appeared three hundred years ago, I would have turned you to stone with one glance of my eyes," said the creature regretfully. "If you had come a hundred years ago, I would have eaten you. But now, I only want to be free to return to my home in the Crystal Mountains."

"Why don't you bite through that rope?" Pilchard said.

"It is a magical rope. Only one knife can cut it, and that knife lies at the bottom of the well behind this tree."

"Hmm," said Pilchard. "If all you really want is to go home, I don't see why I shouldn't give you a hand."

He found the well behind the tree. He put his biggest hook on the end of his fishing line and dropped it into the well. He felt it catch and carefully drew it up. Up came the knife, gleaming and dripping.

With one slash, Pilchard cut through the rope. The basilisk sprang away. It flapped its wings, and the wind of them blew Pilchard flat.

"Free!" roared the creature. "What shall I give you in return for my freedom?"

Pilchard sat up. "You can tell me where to find the Water of Life."

"It lies far to the west," said the basilisk, "on a hill called the Hill of Morna. Around the top of the hill is an iron wall with a pair of iron gates. Inside the wall are four lions guarding a fountain, and from that fountain springs the Water of Life."

"Dear me," said Pilchard. "It sounds hard to get at."

"I will help you," the basilisk said. "Wait here."

It leaped into the air, beating its wings, and flew off. In a few moments, it returned and laid three objects on the ground.

"This," it said, "is the Key That Fits All Locks. It will open the iron gates. This is the Flute That Charms All Beasts. It will charm the lions and put them to sleep. And this is the Bottle That Has No Bottom. No matter how much you put into it, it will always hold more. In it, you can carry away the Water of Life."

On the wind of its wings, it left him.

Pilchard stowed away the three things in his knapsack and plodded on to find the Hill of Morna.

After a time, he came to a valley where a little house stood all alone. It was made of stone, with a red roof, and it was very trim and pretty. In front of it, an old man sat on the ground, sighing and groaning.

"What's the matter?" asked Pilchard.

"Matter?" said the old man. "I built this house for myself, to keep my treasures in. Now I must go away to visit my daughter, and I have lost the key. What am I to do?"

"That's too bad," said Pilchard. He looked at the old man and started to turn away. Then he said to himself, "Surely I can give him a hand?"

"I have a key that will fit all locks," he said. "Let's try it."

He took out the key and tried it in the door. It turned smoothly.

"Now the house is locked," said the old man. "But how will I get in when I come home?"

"You're right," said Pilchard. "You'd better keep the key."

The old man thanked him, and Pilchard went on his way.

He traveled across a wide, grassy plain and passed through a little village. On the other side of the village were hills, and at the foot of the hills he found a little boy crying bitterly.

"What's the matter?" asked Pilchard.

The little boy stopped crying, wiped his nose on his sleeve, and looked up at Pilchard.

"My job is to call the goats home from their pasture every night," he said. "I climb up into the hills and whistle very loudly between my front teeth. The goats hear my whistle and come to me. But now — well, just look."

He opened his mouth. Both his front teeth were gone.

"They both came out," he said. "And until my second teeth grow in, what shall I do?"

"Can't you whistle loudly any other way?" asked Pilchard.

"I don't know how," said the boy.

"Neither do I," said Pilchard. "But maybe I can give you a hand anyway."

He took out the flute. "This is a flute that will charm all beasts," he said. "Let's see if it will charm your goats."

He blew into the flute. Its sweet, clear note filled the evening air. From the hills, the goats came running, flocking close to him.

"Oh, thank you!" said the boy. "But what shall I do tomorrow?"

"You will have the flute," said Pilchard, with a smile.

He went on, traveling westward, and after some days he came to a fine farm. Young wheat sprouted in the fields, and cows grazed in the meadows. A man walked up and down before the farm house, muttering to himself and shaking his head.

"What's the matter?" asked Pilchard.

"I have fifty gallons of milk from my cows," said the farmer, "and it must go to the market. But my old horse is lame and can't pull the wagon. If I don't get the milk to market, I will be ruined. What on earth can I do?"

"I can't pull a wagon loaded with fifty gallons of milk," said Pilchard, "but perhaps I can give you a hand anyway."

He took out the bottle. "This is a bottle which has no bottom," said he. "Let's see if it will hold all your milk."

They went into the barn and began to pour milk into the bottle. Gallon after gallon went in and still there was room for more. At last, all the milk was in the bottle, and Pilchard put the cork in.

"That is a wonderfully convenient bottle," said the farmer wistfully.

"Take it and welcome," Pilchard said.

Off he went again. And soon, before him, rose the green hill which was called the Hill of Morna.

Slowly, he climbed to the top. There he found a pair of iron gates in an iron wall. He looked through the bars and saw four great tawny lions with their chins on their paws. Their golden eyes were wide awake. In the center, a bright fountain of water shot up, and this was the Water of Life.

Pilchard gave a long sigh.

"Even if I didn't have the key," he said, "I might have climbed over the gates. And even if I didn't have the flute, I might have escaped the lions. But I haven't anything to carry away the water in."

He sat down on the grass outside the gates and began to laugh.

"Well, I *am* foolish," he said. "But still, I'm not sorry I gave all those people a hand."

After a while, he noticed something. A thin trickle of water was running along the grass near him. It came from under the iron wall.

"It is the water overflowing from the fountain!" he said to himself.

He got up and began to follow the trickle. It grew wider going down the hill and became a brook. Blue irises rose beside it, and bullrushes grew in it.

At the bottom of the hill, it widened still more into a rushing stream. It flowed over pebbles and among rocks, and willows trailed their leaves in it.

Still, he followed it, until it became a broad river. Boats sailed on it, men fished in it, children swam in it. Clear and sparkling, it flowed on until it swept in a wide bend past Pilchard's own cottage and the village and the town and the king's castle, and on to the sea.

Pilchard was tired and hot and dusty. He stooped and drank a mouthful of water. He felt refreshed and cheerful again. He stood up and marched to the castle.

There sat the king in his silver-walled room on a throne of gold. "Well, Pilchard," said he, "have you found the Water of Life?"

"Yes, Your Majesty, I've found it," said Pilchard.

"Good!" the king said. "Where is it?"

"It's outside your window," said Pilchard. "It is in the river, in the sea, in the streams and the brooks. It gives you health and joy. If you're ill, it makes you feel better. And wherever it is, everything blossoms and is beautiful."

He sat down and told the king all his adventures.

The king began to laugh. And then he said, "Pilchard, you have given everyone a hand. Now, give me your hand."

Pilchard held out his hand and the king clasped it. "From now on," said the king, "I will be your friend, and you may have anything you wish for. Tell me, what would you like most in all the world?"

"To go fishing, Your Majesty," said Pilchard.